POLICE!

Adapted by **Frank Berrios**

Based on the teleplay "Rusty and the Bit Police"
by **Scott Gray**

Illustrated by **Luke Flowers**

 A GOLDEN BOOK • NEW YORK

T#: 565826
rhcbooks.com
ISBN 978-1-5247-7241-3
Printed in the United States of America
10 9 8 7 6 5 4 3 2 1

Ruby and the Bits were playing in the Recycling Yard when they were interrupted by a loud noise.

"Check out the megaphone I mega fixed up for Officer Carl!" said Rusty. "It has three settings: Really Loud; Really, Really Loud; and Really, Really, Really Loud."

Suddenly, they heard another noise. This one came from the street. Rusty and Ruby went to investigate.

Rusty and Ruby spotted Officer Carl in the traffic circle.

"Does he look slightly busier than usual?" asked Ruby.

"Yeah," said Rusty. "That traffic jam is bumper to bumper to bumper to BUMPER!" He pulled out the new and improved megaphone and gave it to Carl.

"My megaphone!" said Officer Carl. "Thanks, guys! The stoplight's broken. It's tough being the only police officer in Sparkton Hills."

Rusty had an idea. "What if you had some new deputies to help you out?"

"New deputies?" asked Officer Carl.

"Yep! Let's get some Bits on the fix!" replied Ruby.

"Deputy Ray, the traffic light is broken!" said Rusty. "We need you to help Officer Carl."

Whirly grabbed Ray and placed him on top of the broken streetlight. Using green, yellow, and red lights, Ray quickly got the cars moving again.

With traffic under control, Officer Carl raced off to his next assignment: helping to get a cat out of a tree.

"Don't worry, little kitty-cat. Remain calm!"
said Officer Carl. "Help has arrived."

Suddenly, a call came over his walkie-talkie.

"Officer Carl, come in! Boater in trouble on
Lake Sprocket!"

"A boater in distress. A kitty-cat in distress.
I can't save them both at the same time!" groaned
Officer Carl.

"We can help!" said Rusty. He strapped a jet pack to Crush. "This will blast you up to that cat, Deputy Crush."

"Then you can carry her down in style," added Ruby.

Zoom! Using the jet pack, Crush easily flew up to the cat.

"Thanks, Deputy Crush!" said Officer Carl.
"Officer Carl is seriously busy," said Rusty.
"I'm glad the Bits could help."
"Maybe they can help the boater, too!"
said Ruby.

At the lake, Officer Carl spotted Sammy out on the water.

"Are you okay?" he called.

"Officer Carl, am I glad to see you!" shouted Sammy. "I ran out of gas!"

"I just need to figure out a way to get out there," replied Officer Carl.

Just then, Whirly arrived.

"Deputy Whirly, we need you to fly out
to Sammy and tow him back to shore.
Can you do it?" Ruby asked.

With a nod, Whirly was off! She used a
cable and hook to latch on to the Jet Ski.

"Whirly to the rescue!" exclaimed Sammy.

Officer Carl received another call over his
walkie-talkie. "There's traffic trouble downtown."
"Traffic? Downtown? But we left Ray there,"
said Rusty.
"Oh, no!" said Ruby. "He must need help!"
"We're on our way!" replied Officer Carl.

When Rusty and Ruby arrived, they saw the problem.
"Ray can't keep up with the traffic!" exclaimed Rusty.
"Where's Officer Carl?" asked one of the drivers.
"We need his help!"
"I'm . . . here!" replied a breathless Officer Carl
as he ran up.

Suddenly, a call came over his walkie-talkie. "Another problem at the kitty tree!"

"The Bits are doing their best," said Rusty. "But it looks like nobody can fill in for you, Officer Carl."

"I just can't get around town fast enough to do everything!" Officer Carl said.

Rusty had an idea. "Ruby, what if there was a way to get Officer Carl anywhere he wanted, super fast?"

"Let's combine it . . . ," began Ruby.

". . . and design it!" finished Rusty.

Rusty and Ruby added jet packs to an old motorcycle and then attached Officer Carl's mega-loud megaphone.

"Modified. Customized. Rustified!" said Rusty proudly. "Introducing the All-Terrain High-Speed Hovercycle 4000!"

Officer Carl couldn't believe his eyes.
"Is it as fast as it looks?" he asked.
"Faster!" replied Rusty.

Officer Carl grabbed his megaphone.

"Don't worry, citizens of Sparkton Hills," he said.
"Officer Carl is here! And now I can fly! *Woo-hoo!*"

He zipped off on his hovercycle. He placed several
traffic signs around the broken streetlight, and soon
the cars were moving again!

Back at the kitty tree, Officer Carl used the hovercycle to go up, up, up. When he was close enough, the kitty-cat hopped onto his helmet. "I have a furry new hat," giggled Officer Carl.

Ruby received an emergency call from Whirly. She needed help pulling the Jet Ski! Officer Carl zoomed to the lake. Using a towline, he pulled Sammy back to shore.

"Thanks for saving me!" said Sammy.
"Let's hear it for the best—and only—police officer in Sparkton Hills: Officer Carl!" added Rusty. Everyone clapped and cheered!

"I couldn't have done it without you—and the Hovercycle 4000!" said Officer Carl. "As a show of thanks, who wants a ride?"

Crush and Whirly bounced with joy.

"Deputy Crush, Deputy Whirly—hop on!" exclaimed Officer Carl.

"Ready? Then away we go!" chuckled Officer Carl.
   It was a wonderful way to end a busy day!